SIMON & SCHUSTER BOOKS FOR YOUNG READERS
An imprint of Simon & Schuster Children's Publishing Division
1230 Avenue of the Americas, New York, New York 10020
Text copyright © 2001 by Douglas Wood
Illustrations copyright © 2001 by Doug Cushman
All rights reserved including the right of reproduction in whole or in part in any form.
SIMON & SCHUSTER BOOKS FOR YOUNG READERS is a trademark of Simon & Schuster.

Book design by Anahid Hamparian
The text of this book is set in 20-pt. Garamond Book.
The illustrations are rendered in pen and ink, watercolors and gouache, and lots of coffee.
Printed in Mexico

10   9   8   7   6   5   4   3   2

Library of Congress Cataloging-in-Publication Data
Wood, Douglas, 1951-
What moms can't do / by Douglas Wood ; pictures by Doug Cushman.
p. cm.
Summary: A child ponders the many problems that mothers must deal
with in the course of a normal day.
ISBN 0-689-83358-X
[1. Mothers—Fiction.] I. Cushman, Doug, ill. II. Title.
PZ7.W84738Whm 2000
[E]—dc21
99-462285

What Moms Can't Do

Also available by Douglas Wood and illustrated by Doug Cushman:

What Dads Can't Do

What Moms Can't Do

by **Douglas Wood**

pictures by **Doug Cushman**

Simon & Schuster Books for Young Readers

New York   London   Toronto   Sydney   Singapore

There are lots of things
that regular people can do
but moms can't.

Moms can't wait …

to wake up kids in the morning.

They can't make the bed
without lots of help.

Moms can never pick out just the right clothes.

And they have trouble keeping things cleaned up.

Moms can't have Yummos with purple
marshmallows for breakfast. Only
coffee, or tea, or yogurt, or bran flakes.
Yuck.

They need a little advice when they're packing lunches.

Moms can't run very fast.

Sometimes moms can't hear themselves think
(whatever that means).

Moms are not good at saying good-bye.

Even to the teacher.

Moms can't push grocery carts fast enough.

And sometimes they need help opening doors.

Moms don't know how to keep
salamanders in their shirts.

Or toads in their pockets.

Moms aren't very good tacklers.

And they can't make a basket on their own.

Moms are easy to squirt,
    but they have a hard time squirting you.

Usually.

Moms really don't like to watch movies by themselves.

And sometimes they need protection
during the scary parts.

They feel much better with someone
on their lap.

Moms can't let go of a hug without a kiss.
Or two.
Or nine.

There are lots of things moms can't do.
More than you can count.
But there's one thing they do better
than almost anyone . . .

and that's
love
you.